CAN YOU FIND ASTERIX?

WHERE IN THE WORLD IS OUR FAMOUS HERO?
SEE IF YOU CAN FIND HIM IN ALL THE ILLUSTRATIONS IN THIS BOOK.
BE PATIENT, KEEP YOUR EYES PEELED, AND GOOD LUCK!

AND IF YOU'RE REALLY GOOD AT IT, THERE'S ANOTHER CHALLENGE.
TURN TO THE END OF THE BOOK TO FIND OUT MORE...

British Library Cataloguing in Publication Data
A catalogue record for this book is available from the British Library
ISBN: 0340 66718 4
© 1998 Les Éditions Albert René / Goscinny-Uderzo.
Published with the authorization of Les Livres du Dragon d'Or
in association with Hodder & Stoughton Ltd.
Printed in Italy.

First published in Great Britain in 1998

Published by Hodder Children's Books a division of Hodder Headline plc
338 Euston Road, London   NW1 3BH

FIND Asterix

HODDER AND STOUGHTON
LONDON   SYDNEY   AUCKLAND

THE VILLAGE OF INDOMITABLE GAULS
THE YEAR IS 50BC. AND THE FAMOUS GAULISH VILLAGE IS STILL HOLDING OUT AGAINST THE INVADERS. BUT WHERE IS ASTERIX, THE MOST FAMOUS GAUL OF ALL?

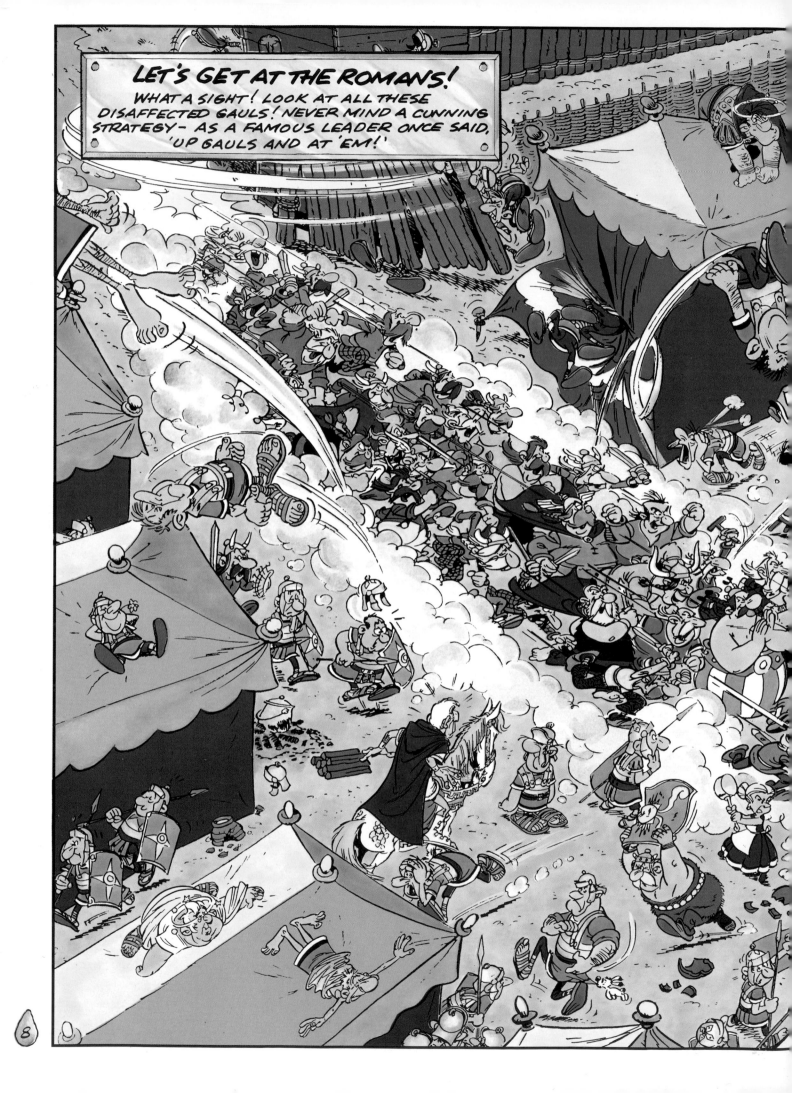

9

ALL FAIR AND SQUARE

...OR AT LEAST, WELL-COVERED. OBELIX IS CHALLENGING ALL GLADIATORS TO A BOXING MATCH AT CONDATUM FAIR. HE'LL BE PLEASED AS PUNCH TO SEE THEM!

15

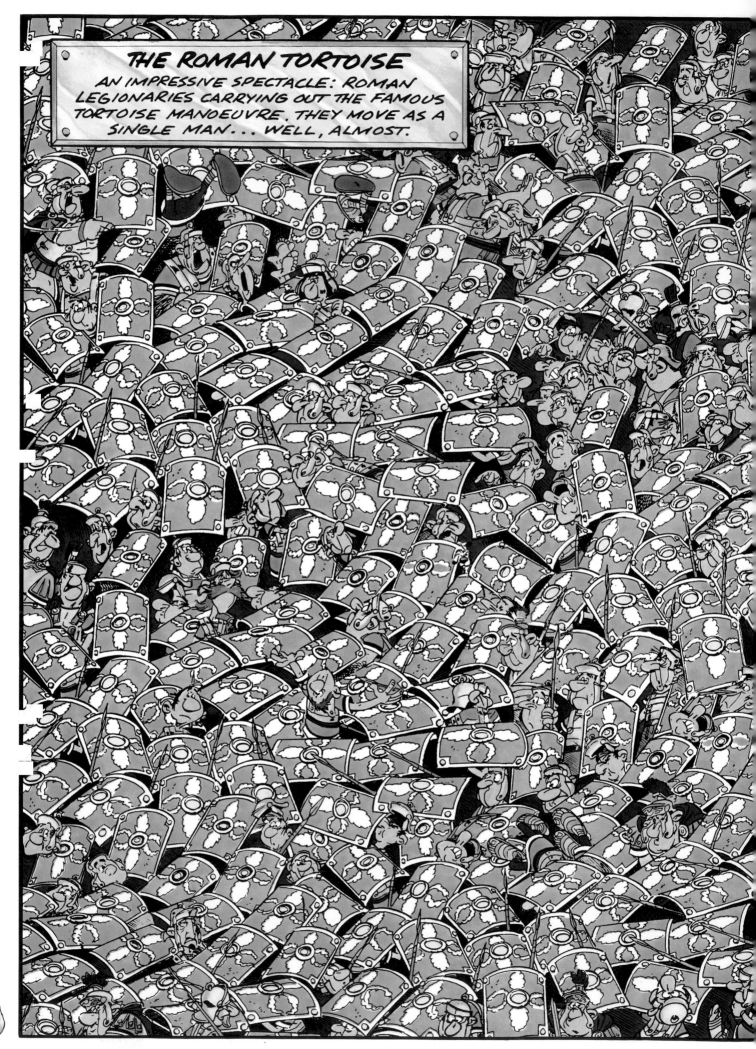

THE ROMAN TORTOISE

AN IMPRESSIVE SPECTACLE: ROMAN LEGIONARIES CARRYING OUT THE FAMOUS TORTOISE MANOEUVRE. THEY MOVE AS A SINGLE MAN... WELL, ALMOST.

A GREAT SITE FOR SORE EYES

A TEMPLE IS BEING BUILT IN ALEXANDRIA, RIGHT UNDER CLEOPATRA'S FAMOUS NOSE. OF COURSE, THE SITE IS A MODEL OF ANCIENT EGYPTIAN EFFICIENCY.

THE BANQUET
THIS IS THE END - WELL, IT WILL BE IF YOU CAN'T FIND ASTERIX! THE TRADITIONAL BANQUET WITH ROAST BOAR AND GAGGED BARD WOULDN'T BE COMPLETE WITHOUT HIM.

THE END

WELL DONE! SO YOU FOUND ASTERIX
IN ALL 12 PICTURES IN THIS BOOK.
BUT CAN YOU DO EVEN BETTER?
IF YOU WANT TO FIND OUT, TRY PLAYING
THE GAME OF
THE CHIEFTAIN'S CHALLENGE
THE CHIEFTAIN'S CHALLENGE CUP OF GAUL
IS HIDDEN IN ONE OF THE
TWELVE SCENES IN THIS BOOK...

IF YOU CAN FIND IT,
YOU'RE THE **CHAMPION!**
(AND IF YOU'D LIKE TO COMPETE
WITH YOUR FRIENDS
DON'T FORGET TO TIME YOURSELVES, TO SEE
WHO FINDS THE CUP FASTEST.)
GOOD LUCK, BY TOUTATIS!